BREAD & WATER

FRANCISCO ANTONIO MIRANDA

authorHOUSE

AuthorHouse™
1663 Liberty Drive
Bloomington, IN 47403
www.authorhouse.com
Phone: 833-262-8899

© 2024 Francisco Antonio Miranda. All rights reserved.

No part of this book may be reproduced, stored in a retrieval system, or transmitted by any means without the written permission of the author.

Published by AuthorHouse   10/25/2024

ISBN: 979-8-8230-3085-4 (sc)
ISBN: 979-8-8230-3084-7 (e)

Library of Congress Control Number: 2024920928

Print information available on the last page.

Any people depicted in stock imagery provided by Getty Images are models, and such images are being used for illustrative purposes only.
Certain stock imagery © Getty Images.

This book is printed on acid-free paper.

Because of the dynamic nature of the Internet, any web addresses or links contained in this book may have changed since publication and may no longer be valid. The views expressed in this work are solely those of the author and do not necessarily reflect the views of the publisher, and the publisher hereby disclaims any responsibility for them.

CONTENTS

1 1
2 7
3 11
4 15
5 19
6 23
7 29
8 41
9 51
10 59
11 75

I

A mysterious and what seems to be a wealthy man is driving an expensive car through a marvelous neighborhood. He pulls up to a magnificent home, and before getting out of his car, he makes a phone call to a very sinister man. He instructs him that it's time they eat, feed the pigs.

"Indeed, sir, with pleasure," the sinister man replies. A short while after the call, the sinister man enters a grocery store and walks down the aisles revealing only his dark, warn-out boots. Then he makes an abrupt stop in front of the display of bread. Reaching out, he snatches up two loaves of bread with a pair of creepy hands.

At that exact same time, the luxurious mystery man is in his kitchen grabbing a loaf of bread himself.

After retrieving the bread, the ominous man heads toward the water aisle. He grabs a gallon with his available hand and proceeds to the checkout area.

Simultaneously, the wealthy unnamed man is stacking himself a meaty sandwich for lunch. His paid help has already checked out and loaded his truck and is on his way to complete his orders given by the man we only know as the unknown man on the other side of the phone. After about a thirty-minute drive, the hired hand pulls up to what looks like a deserted warehouse. And definitely feels that way. He parks on the outer side of the fence, gets out of his truck, and takes out the bread and water, what many would agree is less than groceries. He walks the remainder distance on foot. The sinister man arrives at the entrance of the building.

Unlocking several locks, he opens up a big, swinging metal doorway that leads to a piece of hell on earth. As he closes the door behind himself, a glimmer of light shines on him revealing his face for the first time. It is a face filled without guilt or remorse, perfect for the circumstances at hand. A very dark task indeed, especially having come from what seemed to be a very accomplished and successful man on the other end of a phone conversation.

After locking himself inside the warehouse, the

newly revealed man picks up the loaves of bread and water and starts to walk toward the back of the dilapidated building where he encounters another heavy door secured by multiple locks. He drops his grocery items onto the ground and unlocks the locks one at a time. The first one is a deadbolt, which he clicks open. The second one is a latch, which he slides back. The third is a padlock, which he snaps open. With all locks open, he slowly opens the heavy steel door, which is difficult enough for a single person to open. As he opens the door slowly, a glimmering light emerges. A brightness glows from the inside looking like a chance of hope. After opening it just a little bit, he notices that it is safe to open it completely. Then he kicks it wide open. The back of the door slams into the wall making a cracking loud sound.

With the door opened all the way, a beam of light focuses on three terrified, and what appear to be malnourished, young ladies. Two of them appear to be in worse shape than the third one. "It's feeding time, you pigs," he says. He throws the bread and water directly at them in an expression of hate. He turns and slams the door shut, leaving them inside. He secures all locks, dusts his hands off, and tells himself, *Job well done.* He laughs all the way out of the building to his car. After getting in his vehicle, he secures himself inside by locking his doors, putting on his seatbelt, and places his pistol on the passenger's seat. He immediately calls his boss to inform him all is well. The boss replies, "That should hold them off for a while. Good job. I'll come by later to pay you in person. Then we can talk more about the next steps ahead."

2

A loving couple, Eddy and Paula, met seven years ago. With so much in common, and only two years apart in age, they both felt compatible with each other. One of the most important things they had in common was their less-than-perfect health. Caring for one another mentally and spiritually was more important to them than physical attraction, but that was there too. The only difference was they were both in poor shape and overweight. Nevertheless, they were both full of joy. They believed they were meant to be together. Some would even say they were soulmates. They started climbing the ladder of life together. Eddy was very smart. He had earned his master's degree, and he had landed a six-figure job to support them. Paula, although she did not have a job, was also highly educated. She did not need a job because her love, Eddy, was not insistent about it. They moved in together and settled down over time.

Eddy thinks there is only one thing missing. *Marriage*, he says to himself. So one day he leaves work early to go ring shopping. This is an enlightening experience as he gets a feeling for how much money it's going to take to get a suitable ring. So, he doesn't purchase a ring right away. Instead, after working for a decent amount of time at his job, he feels a bit more secure financially, and he feels he can afford an expensive, gorgeous diamond ring for Paula. This is a ring that, in his mind, she will definitely love. He believes she could not say no to his proposal.

A week passes, and he pops the question. "Paula, you're the love of my life and my best friend. During these last seven years, I have felt like I been floating on a cloud with you. And every day we get closer to heaven on earth. There is only one more thing that can make this more magical." Eddy gets down on one knee and pulls out the ring from his pocket. He asks Paula, "Will you marry me?"

Paula says yes with a big smile. Tears flow down her cheeks. Eddy stands up and gives his finance a big hug and a kiss, and he tells Paula he loves her.

"I love you too, Eddy," Paula says as she stares mesmerized at her ring. She is pleased that Eddy picked it out for her.

3

As newlyweds, Eddy and Paula develop a relationship that progresses along as that of any other married loving couple. They are each happy in life and even happier as husband and wife. They are comfortable with their day-to-day routine as soulmates. Paula is less than a stay-at-home wife. Seeing as she is unfruitful, and the two of them form a small, child-free family. This doesn't bother Eddy that much as he is happy being alone with his wife. On the other hand, Paula has a lot of time to reflect on life being a stay-at-home wife. Consciously she thinks nothing negative. She continues to try to be a happy housewife. Eddy sees their life as perfection. They have everything they need; and wanting for nothing.

Eddy continues on as always, but Paula's subconscious mind hints to her that life could be so much different. One morning after Eddy has gone to work, Paula awakens with an epiphany. Soon after thinking things over all day long, she manifests the idea into reality. Her idea is to get in shape and start to live a healthier life. When Eddy arrives home from work and walks into the house, he finds Paula doing aerobics in front of the TV. Following their usual routine, he has brought home dinner for both of them. Tonight is Chinese takeout—enough for a family of four, which is a typical meal in their household. He takes it to the dining area, sets it down on the table, and then walks over to Paula. He says, "I brought your favorite—sesame chicken."

Paula replies, "Thanks, Eddy, but today is the day that I start to eat healthier. And I'm also starting an exercise regimen." Paula asked Eddy for his support and invites him to come along with her so they can embark on this journey as a couple.

"Easier said than done," says Eddy. And under his breath he says, "I'm not the one who obviously woke up today with an epiphany." He thinks to himself, *I just wanted to get off work, bring some dinner home for us, eat with you, cuddle up on the couch, and watch our favorite shows together.* But seeing that Paula has different plans, he respects her decision and politely takes the food into the kitchen. He makes a plate and watches TV alone. Eddy decides that day will not be the day he starts on his wife's new path in life. But tells her to keep it up and says that he is proud of her. And he plans to join her soon. Paula is excited with Eddy's response and smiles at him.

4

The months fly by, and suddenly an entire year has come and gone. It seems like a lifetime to Paula. She has transformed into an absolutely gorgeous woman. Overnight, she has started to attract various members of the opposite sex. She has accomplished a lifetime achievement in just one short year, and that effort has come with a great reward. Sadly, Eddy never joined her journey to new health and new beginnings. And Paula lost attraction for Eddy almost immediately.

With no love lost in her relationship and a new outlook on life, Paula divorces Eddy. Eddy steps out of the relationship determined to be happy no matter the situation. He looks at this as a short-term marriage. They have no kids, and he still has a great job. He wants to believe everything is okay. He looks at his life as a win-win situation. But after a short while being alone, twenty-four hours starts to feel like forty-eight hours, forty-eight hours starts to feel like a week, a week feels like a month, and a month feels like a year. He realizes he misses the companionship he had with Paula. Knowing that it's over and final, he doesn't look back; rather, he looks to the future and moves forward on his own new journey in life.

While Paula's new life is filled with positivity, Eddy's is the complete opposite. He thinks that going out on the weekends, getting drunk, and spending his hard-earned money to treat himself to new adventures will help him; in fact, these activities cause more conflict in his life. As he heads on a downward spiral, Eddy explores new experiences—gambling, drinking alcohol, taking drugs, and engaging with known prostitutes. With this new lifestyle, he is exposed to new surroundings and new individuals. Many of these individuals are attached to various parts of the murky underground, and they quickly befriend Eddy. They even give him a nick name—Eddy Money—because he never negotiates the price. And he even is willing to pay a premium for whatever he wants from his new friends and associates, especially one individual who goes by the name of Two-Tone Tony. He got that name for wearing silver and gold jewelry at the same time. But to the cops he is known as Two-Bit Tony. And not to be confused with the wise guy that goes by Tony Two Tone, who got his name for always being tanned from the waist up, and legs white as snow.

Nevertheless, Eddy and Two-Tone Tony became tight. Two-Tone runs multiple women and introduces Eddy to a couple exclusive ladies whom he is now seeing on a regular basis and lining Two-Tone's pockets up at the same time. This doesn't bother Eddy at all because he is filling the void of emptiness that he still has inside after his breakup and divorce with his ex-wife Paula. Eddy frequents these women on a regular basis. With a mixture of hard drugs and alcohol, he is numb to his pain. Surprisingly, he is still able to maintain his job in a professional manner during the day. Sadly, he does not realize the consequences he could suffer that could lead to vicious ways.

5

Monday comes fast for Eddie after one of his drunken and drugged weekends fueled by lust and sex with gorgeous women provided by Two-Tone. The party's over; he must go back to work and play the part that provides what is needed for Eddy to continue on the roller-coaster life he has chosen.

As usual, on this Monday, the start of a new week, Eddy is pretty disciplined and will remain so for the rest of the week. Eight hours pass, and

Eddy clocks out for the day. Following his usual routine, he finds himself at his favorite Chinese restaurant. Not having a reason to take food home for a significant other, he eats there alone where he is also known and well liked by all the employees. Eddy looks down at his plate and starts to eat. He suddenly looks up to see his ex-wife, Paula, walking in. She is still as beautiful as she was the day she left him. By her side, holding her hand, walks her boyfriend, her young, fit trainer. Eddy immediately angles his head down so she won't detected him. He realizes that the hostess who greeted them is someone who might recognize her as his previous wife.

After Paula and her boyfriend are seated, Eddy quickly puts money down on the table and generously leaves more than expected as a tip. He feels almost in a joyful way, experiencing happiness for a second just seeing someone he loved more than anything. And never thought he would see again. But that happiness lasts only as long as it took him to make it to the exit. He says to himself on the way out, *It must be that bitch's diet cheat day if she's eating here. It's the same food I brought home for us on the first day of her transformation. She refused it then, and she's eating it on the first day I see her again after the divorce.*

By the time Eddy makes it to his car, he is furious. While he sits in the driver seat, his eyes well up with tears. One tear rolls down to his upper lip. He licks it off with his tongue. It is a bitter tear, wept for the destructive life he has chosen after his devoice from Paula. He spits the salty taste out of his mouth, grabs his phone, and starts to block all contacts that he has made in any negative way. Seeing as the majority of them always contacts him first, which makes it almost imposable to break free from the addictive lifestyle that he has chosen. As he drives away, he feels good about himself and indulges himself in positive self-talk.

Over the next few weeks, Eddy starts using his money wisely, eating healthful foods, and joining a fitness club. With preeminent trainers on his side, Eddy starts his own transformation.

6

Eddy focuses on the core of his new center of attention. He maintains a workout routine and a new diet regimen. He also maintains a positive mindset, and it all starts to pay off. Coworkers actually compliment him on his discipline and hard work. His physical appearance has changed dramatically. This makes Eddy very happy with himself, but it is short lived as he falls back into depression and anxiety. He just can't get over losing the love of his life to someone he could have been. If he only had the passion then that he has now.

His new lifestyle seems like passion and desire, but in actuality, it is the fire that burns with hatred that is encouraging him to exceed. Strangely enough, Eddy is pleased with the progress in his own way, but he is not quite there yet. With mixed emotions, he tries to stay focused on the positive aspects of his life over the negative ones. He carries on.

A year has passed since the beginning of Eddy's commitment, and it has been a good year indeed. With hard work and dedication, Eddy has accomplished his goal of extreme physical transformation. He is mesmerized by his own reflection in the mirror.

With his new health and good looks, Eddy decides to go out for a night on the town to test his new look and to see if he has the charm to match.

He feels he can finally leave Paula in the past where she belongs. Going all out on his special night with no limit of spending on his mind, he reserves a table and orders champagne and several varieties of top-shelf bottles for himself at one of the most highly rated and exclusive nightclubs in the city. He even hires a luxury limo and has the driver drop him off. And will pick him up when he is ready to go home.

The limo pulls up to the red-carpet entrance, and the driver gets out and opens the door for him. The place is crowded and everyone there instantly has their eyes on Eddy. He notices one gorgeous young lady in particular who seems to have a sparkle in her eye for him. Her engagement with him makes it easy for Eddy to extend his hand toward her. She immediately extends her hand to Eddy. Hand in hand, they walk into the club together. Eddy softly whispers compliments on her beauty as they enter. That's as far as the conversation goes that night. She clearly has chosen Eddy for the night, and they both let their physical attraction for one another do all the talking. The alcohol, the lights, the music, and the dancing all intensify their relationship. They even make out on the dance floor. After the music slows down, they head back to Eddy's reserved table where he has invited several people to indulge in all he has to offer. He does not mind because they are all friends of his new encounter. Eddy and his lady friend take one last drink before heading out of the club. They make a toast to each other before they exit the building. They are met by Eddy's driver who greets them and opens the limo door. He asks Eddy, "Is there anywhere in particular that you would like to go?"

Eddy says, "No. Just drive."

After the driver shuts the door, isolating them both together, the sexual tension they experienced in the club starts all over again. Without hesitation, she takes off her top, reveling what Eddy's been focusing on half the night. Eddy sits her on his lap facing him. He slowly lifts her skirt up and seductively rubs her butt. He then rips off her panties, pulls down his pants, and attaches himself to her. Then he fastens her in for the ride by wrapping her legs around his back locking them together securely.

They make passionate love in the same position all the way back to Eddy's house. There, the lovemaking heats up in every imaginable way. They try to stay awake, but finally pass out unintentionally.

After the moon goes down, the sun comes up and shines brightly into Eddy's bedroom, striking him in the face, waking him out his slumber. He is greeted by the warmth of the sun but falls short in the comfort of his companion from the night before.

She has left no note—no name and no number. Eddy has been introduced to the world of the one-night stand.

Eddy doesn't know exactly what he is looking for at the moment. He keeps his head down and continues focusing on his job as well as keeping up with the new lifestyle he's adapted to.

7

After staying focused for so long, even after Eddy's amazing night out and one night stand, the loneliness and depression sets back in and his faith starts to slip. That's when a small burst of hope emerges for Eddy. It dawns on him that, as attractive as he is, it might be easier to attract those he perceives as less desirable. This causes him to believe that he has an advantage. With that glimmer of hope, Eddy believes he still has a chance for love again. Indeed, Eddy's ex-wife,

Paula, had been overweight when they met, and she was the love of his life. That thought boggles Eddy's mind as he remembers how much in love they were and then how gorgeous she became and left him in the end.

As Eddy's faith drops, he turns sinister. He revels in his good looks and minimum charm and cultivates his new confidence born with hate. He makes his decision right then to be a wolf in sheep's clothing. He starts to construct new ideas and plans. One plan is to hunt and prey on overweight women. But for starters, he looks for an abandoned warehouse that he can rent. After looking for about a week, Eddy has a stroke of luck. He finds the perfect building for his purposes. Lucky for Eddy, the building was inherited by some punk kid who is a month away from selling it and getting ripped off in the process.

The kid is happy to rent it to Eddy and become a slum lord at the same time.

Even though Eddy senses the landlord's situation and intention, he pays the kid three months' rent in advance. With no questions or concerns, the kid excepts the payments. After taking possession of the building, Eddy puts a no trespassing sign on the fence and installs locks on the gate. After Eddy is sure his new place is secure, he goes back to work and returns to his normal routine. Over the next few days, he searches for workers to construct a room in his new warehouse.

While Eddy's at work, he becomes more and more focused on his new idea, and he begins to look online for contractors who can meet him at his warehouse after work so he can move to phase two of his plan. Because Eddy's job is at the higher end of the company's scale, one day at work without any of the company's work being done is barely recognized, but even luckier for Eddy, he finds what he is looking for the same day—an independent contractor who is wide open for work.

Eddy sends the address of the warehouse to this contractor and tells him to meet him there in the evening. He tells him to bring his tools and be ready to work. He will be burning the midnight oil! To encourage the contractor, Eddy promises that there will be a bonus if he can expedite the accomplishment of Eddy's plan.

The contractor finishes up in just two days and tells Eddy he is happy to receive the promised bonus. But Eddy is even happier because he can now move on to the next part of his plan. Out of curiosity, the contractor asks Eddy, "What are your plans with the building?"

Eddy quickly turns to him and says, "If you must know, I'm preparing the building to be a haunted house for Hallowe'en.

The contractor says under his breath, "More like a haunting house."

Eddy responds, "Are you trying to say something?"

The contractor says, "I was just going to say that's a great idea, and you know where you can find me if you need more work done."

Eddy says, "That will be all. Thank you."

The contractor exits the warehouse, but not without getting the chills first. Eddy pays the contractor no mind and moves toward the next part of his plan.

After a long week of hard work and being a

square, tax-paying citizen, Eddy rejoices that the weekend is here. He is ready. Dressed to impress and smelling his best, he goes out on the night scene to see what is in store for him. Eddy must make sure he has the upper hand during his search. He picks a place where he is sure to find a variety of women so that he can blend in nicely and work all angles until he finds what he is looking for.

Eddy steps into the club looking amazing. Several gorgeous opportunities immediately give him the eye. But he already knows how that sort of thing works out. He is no longer interested, and he keeps his mind focused on the task at hand. He casually walks up to the bar and orders a drink. As he turns and takes his first sip, Eddy sees a woman who cannot be denied or ignored because of her size. Eddy makes eye contact with her right before she is approached by another man, but not before he gives her a signal to let him call her.

Eddy turns back to the bar and continues to sip his drink. He is met there soon after by another attractive but overweight lady. Eddy greets her by introducing himself. "Hi. My name is Eddy. What's your name, gorgeous?"

She replies, "Let's start with drinks first."

Eddy says, "Perfect. I'm just about done with this one. What are you having, sweetheart?"

She replies, "Martini. Extra olives."

Eddy says, "I think I'll have the same. Bartender, two please."

After receiving their drinks, they toast to a good night. She has consumed only half of her martini, and she seems mesmerized by her conversation with Eddy. She asks him, "Do you want to leave with me?"

Eddy says, "Sure. I know the perfect place."

She says, "Great. I'll be right back, handsome. Then we can go."

Eddy is not aware that the girl he had flirted with first is waiting for her opportunity to approach him. Before Eddy's date returns, she slips him her phone number and disappears back into the ambience of the club.

"Okay. I'm back," says Eddy's date.

Eddy replies, "Let's go, baby." When they get to Eddy's car, he opens the door for her and then gets in beside her.

She says, "Thank you for opening my door. This is a nice car. Where are we going?"

Eddy replies, "Sit back and relax, baby. I have to

make one stop before I drive us back to my spot. But I guarantee this will be a night that you'll never forget."

She replies with a big smile.

"Oh yeah," continues Eddy, "do me a favor, baby, and turn off your phone for me. I don't want any disturbances while we are together."

She replies, "Yes, baby. Anything you say."

They pull up to Eddy's warehouse. On the outside, it is extremely dilapidated, and she does not hesitate to mention it to him. Eddy tells her that he is renovating the building from the inside out. "Let's go in. I'll show you!"

Eddy gets out of his car and opens the gate. While Eddy is opening the gate. All she can think about is the amazing sex that she's hoping to have tonight, and maybe he wants to start here. Eddy gets back into the car and drives into the parking lot. He asks her if she's ready and she replies, "So ready!"

"Good," says Eddie. "Get out of the car, bitch, and come check it out." Being spoken to like that kind of turns her on, so she voluntarily follows Eddy inside to see if her expectations are right.

As they walk deep into the building, the only light comes from the moon shining through the broken glass windows. It is then that fear first strikes her. Only Eddy knows the layout of the building, so she continues to follow him, but now she does so in fear.

She has no clue that Eddy is leading her to his newly created dungeon and torture chamber. As they both get closer, Eddy mumbles to himself, "You want to leave me, bitch? I loved you. And you left me all alone. Now you're gonna be all alone."

Then Eddy yells out, "You fat bitch! You want to get skinny and fucking leave me?"

By this time they have made it to the open door of Eddy's secret room. She frantically responds. "No, Eddy. No! That's not me. I'm not skinny."

Eddy quickly pushes her inside and locks the door from the outside. She starts to yell and scream. Eddy turns away and says, "You will be sooner or later." Her cries for help fade away the closer Eddy gets to the exit. He comments to himself while he looks at the exterior of the building, "I just need to figure out what I want to do with you. Maybe I'll get a couple more and call up Two-Tone.

8

Eddy wakes up the following morning after a great night's sleep. He had got his weekend started early by going out Friday night. He has two more days off to contemplate his next move. He is not really worried too much about the girl from last night. He knows that she is secure due to the excellent work he had contracted for, especially after offering such a generous incentive to the contractor.

So Eddy is not in any hurry to get up. While he

lies in bed, he remembers the other girl he had met at the club, and he remembers that she had given him her number. Eddy hops quickly out of bed and checks his pants pockets. He finds her note, looks at it, and says to himself in an evil manner, "You want to leave me, bitch? I'm coming for you now."

Eddy grabs his phone and punches in her number as he changes his demeanor into that of a Casanova. The phone rings only twice before she answers. "Hello?" she says.

"Hey, gorgeous," Eddy replies.

"I'm glad you called," she says.

"Of course I'm assuming you know who this is," Eddy says.

"Yes," she says. "I gave you my number at the club when your girlfriend went to the restroom."

"That was not my girlfriend." says Eddie. "I did

leave the club with her, but she isn't my type. I like you. Besides, I think she got locked up last night. Never mind her. Let's have dinner tonight."

She replies, "Definitely. I'll send you my address. You can pick me up."

"Okay, baby. I'll be there at seven."

"Okay. I can't wait!"

After hanging up the phone Eddy says to himself, *Me neither!* Eddy has several hours till he has to get ready for his date, so he goes to the gym to train so he can maintain his new physique and perhaps to discover a new target.

Eddy pulls up to the gym, gets out of his car, and walks into the gym. He almost immediately becomes the focus of some of the most attractive women in the gym. But he ignores the gawks from the beautiful women and heads straight to an empty rowing machine next to one on which an overweight but cute young lady is working out at.

Eddy sits down on the machine and starts to row. The young lady next to him soon feels out of place because she is surrounded by so many people who are in great shape. She gets up and starts to walk away. Eddy sees his chance and acts on it. He stops her and says, "Hi! My name is Eddy. Nice to meet you. I couldn't help but notice the way you were using that machine. Looks to me that you might be a beginner at this."

The young lady smiles and blushes. "Is it that obvious?" My name is Michelle."

Eddy replies, "Not really. I just wanted to get your attention before you started walking away. I know it might be hard to believe just by looking at me, but I used to be in very poor shape. I was obese."

Michelle is amazed that Eddy has even stopped her to talk. She takes advantage of it by listening to Eddy speak. "Wow!" she replies, "You look amazing."

"Thank you," said Eddy. "If you like, I can help you look amazing too." Eddy told her about his building that he has just rented and is in the process of making it into a gym. Michelle is intrigued by Eddy's plan. Michelle says, "Yes I would like that. Thank you."

Eddy gives Michelle his number and tells her to call him the next day so they can work out together. "And afterwards I can show you my building, and you can give me your opinion on it."

Michelle replies, "Yes, that sounds like fun. It's a date." Michelle walks away as Eddy continues his workout, but not before saying to himself in a sinister way, *A date indeed. In fact, mark that date down on the calendar as the last day anyone will see you again as a ugly, fat bitch!* Eddy rows for his allotted time on the machine and heads to the sauna. Where he finishes up his workout for the day, he goes home to shower and prepare for his dinner date that evening.

The evening arrives quickly, and Eddy is ready. He has dressed to impress and again is smelling his best. He almost believes he is going out on a legitimate date with someone he's trying to impress enough that she will want to see him again. But that's not the case with Eddy; he believes he needs only one chance to achieve his goal. "So here goes nothing," says Eddy on his way out the door. He gets into his car and sits there for a while before leaving. But soon he is on his way to pick up his next victim. Eddy calculates the route from his house to hers and thinks about the nearest nicest restaurant. He takes into consideration the distance from his warehouse where he intends to end up at the end of the night.

With Eddy's calculations for driving from location to location, he figures the night should last an estimated time of two and a half hours. Everything is going as planned, and he will be able to get to bed early so he can be up early for his Sunday funday date with Michelle. "Here we go," Eddy says as he starts his car and follows the directions provided by his car's built-in navigation system. He is meeting his scheduling expectations so far as he pulls up to his date's house. With no hesitation, she is already outside waiting for him. Eddy pulls up beside her and rolls down his window. "Did someone order a one-way ticket to hell? I'm joking of course."

She replies, "Stop kidding."

As she gets in the car, Eddy introduces himself. "By the way, my name is Eddy. I never got your name, sweetheart."

"Oh, my name is Paula."

An extreme sensation of warmth hurtles through Eddy's insides when he hears her name. After Eddy comes to realization, he replies, "Is that so? Well, I'm just going to have to treat you like a Paula."

"What does that mean, Eddy?"

"You soon shall find out." After that remark, Eddy turns the subject back to the evening's plans. "Do you like Italian food?"

"Yes! It's my favorite," says Paula.

"Great. I have a *paisan* who owns a fantastic Italian restaurant, and he has reserved a special table for us." That is just a lie of course. Eddy is not even Italian; neither does he know the owner of the restaurant where they will be dinning. Eddy is just trying to sound like a big shot so his date will be confident in him. Paula seems satisfied with Eddy's recommendations. She even mentions that she hopes she won't get too full on bread before the main course. Eddy says, "Eat plenty. You're going to need it were we're going after dinner. I have a feeling you're going to be burning it all off soon."

As they pull up to the valet parking at the restaurant, Eddy looks at Paula with a handsome smile. "Now, let's go eat andiamo a mangiare" says Eddy. As they walk in holding hands, Eddy stops suddenly and asks Paula to remind him after dinner that he needs to make one quick stop before their next destination.

"Sure," Paula replies. Eddy thanks her by kissing her on her lips. She blushes afterwards.

As their fine dining experience comes to a conclusion, both Eddy and Paula are too full for dessert, but that does not stop Eddy from asking for some extra bread to go. "I love this bread," he tells Paula.

"Yes, it's great," she says.

Eddy replies, "I'm glad you like it. I'm getting some for you ... I mean us."

Paula looks slightly distraught after hearing Eddy's mixed words, but she immediately puts her feelings out of her mind. As they leave the restaurant and get into Eddy's car, she reminds him about the stop he has to make. Eddy thanks her for reminding him and says, "Gee, I'm glad you reminded me. I almost forgot." He rolls his eyes. They snuggle in the car. Eddy puts on some romantic jazz music. That combined with the good food and vino puts plump Paula into a restful slumber.

9

Eddy wakes up in his bed after a peaceful night of sleep.

At the same time, Paula wakes up to the horrific screams of Eddy's first capture. Luckily for Eddy and unluckily for Paula, he had successfully placed Paula in captivity the night before. It had all been quiet because she had remained in deep sleep and his first, unnamed victim had been passed out as well. She was in a state of exhaustion because of the emotional stress and physical fatigue not to mention starvation.

The captured woman immediately ignores her situation when she notices that food has been placed next to Paula. She leaps toward it and scarfs it down without remorse. She even punches Paula in the face because she doesn't realize that they are both now prisoners.

Paula finds herself huddled in a corner of the room in confusion.

Eddy is blind to the conditions in which he has left the two women. At the moment, he is interested only in his next endeavor, which he calls Sunday funday.

Right on time, Michelle calls Eddy shortly after he wakes up. But she is not calling with the intent to go out as planned; rather, she has called to reschedule. Eddy is immediately disappointed but shows no signs of it. Instead, he turns the Casanova charm on. He sends a shirtless photo of himself to Michelle hoping to let the image of his body speak for him.

As they are speaking on the phone, Michelle receives the photo but does not mention it to Eddy. Instead, she instantly changes her mind and tells Eddy, "Yes, let's meet at the gym, and then you can show me your place." Michelle apologizes to Eddy. "I'm sorry, Eddy. Anything you want. I know you are just trying to help me."

Eddy thanks her and says, "You won't regret it." The conversation ends there.

After hanging up, Michelle smiles and gets ready to meet Eddy.

Not much later, they both pull up to the gym at

the same time. Michelle gets out of her car thinking she will walk in the gym with Eddy. But Eddy has changed his plans and is confident that Michelle will agree. Eddy remains in his car, so Michelle walks over to him. Eddy rolls down his window, and compliments Michelle on her looks. Michelle blushes. Eddy then tells her to get in because he thinks it would be better to show her his place first. Michelle agrees and gets into Eddy's car. Eddy leans over and gives Michelle a big kiss on her lips and tells her she is going to really like this place. He encourages her to express any opinion of it that she has.

Michelle is content for the moment and is giving Eddy her undivided attention and total trust. Eddy pulls up to his warehouse, and Michelle says, "This is quite a scary place." Eddy takes control of the situation by pulling down his pants.

Michelle is shocked at first, but she says, "Now that's a much better view." She lowers her head toward Eddy's lap.

Eddy enjoys the pleasure Michelle provides and says quietly, "Scary! You'll see scary soon." After an explosive finish, both Eddy and Michelle are equally satisfied. They get out of Eddy's vehicle and walk up to the gate that surrounds the warehouse. Eddy unlocks the lock, opens the gate, and they walk into the parking lot together hand and hand. As they get closer to the building, Michelle starts to make an observation about what she is seeing. Eddy pays her no mind as they come to the loading-bay door entrance. He tells her to wait there so he can go in through the side door.

From inside the building, Eddy pulls down on the chain slowly opening up the loading-bay door.

Standing outside, Michelle sees the huge garage door opening up at a slow pace. It comes to a stop at a point right about her height. A big cloud of dust billows out over the threshold. Eddy emerges as the dust settles. "Come in, Michelle," Eddy says. "Let me take you to my newly renovated room."

Michelle walks in slowly wondering if she made the right choice to come. As she stands in the center of the large space, she hears frantic cries echoing in the distance. Michelle immediately turns around and starts to run for the exit, but Eddy is prepared. When Michelle turned away from Eddy, she was unaware that he had pulled out a head cover. He successfully puts it over her head and secures it in place by pulling a drawstring. Even that does not deter Michelle from trying to run away as fast as she can. But she comes to an abrupt stop when she bumps her head on an old bit of machinery that was left behind by the previous owner. Michelle is knocked out cold.

Eddy laughs and laughs, holding his arms down at his sides and pointing his head up toward the ceiling. After Eddy's initial amusement passes, he walks over to Michelle and checks her pulse. Michelle is alive but unconscious. Eddy looks at the situation as a success nevertheless. He drags Michelle by her arms the short distance to the secure room that he has built. He then lays her down so he can unlock the door and check to make sure it is safe to open.

All the while, the two women inside are exhausted by starvation and the effort of screaming for help. They are unable to take advantage of the open door and attempt an escape. Eddy grabs Michelle again and drags her inside. He drops her onto the floor and quickly exits the room, securing the door behind him.

The weekend is concluded, and Monday starts a new week. Eddy rolls into work like a man who has just been promoted. One employee compliments Eddy after seeing him out over the weekend. "Hey, Eddy, I saw you out this weekend. She's cute!"

Eddy mumbles, "I have her on a weight-loss program. Soon you won't even recognize her."

His coworker replies, "What did you say, Eddy?"

Eddy replies, "Thanks. I had three this weekend. Which one are you talking about?"

His coworker is insulted. "Hey, I was trying to give you a compliment, Eddy. You know what? Go fuck yourself!"

Eddy smirks as he walks away talking to himself. "I just might. But first I need to call an old friend."

10

A phone rings. It is picked up by Eddy's old friend by the name Two-Tone Tony. "Hello. Who's this?"

Eddy replies, "Is this Two-Tone?"

"Yeah, motherfucker, this is Two-Tone. Who's this?"

"This is Eddy, man."

"This ain't no fucking Eddy, man. You don't sound like the Eddy I know."

"I look different too. You got some girls for me, Tone?" They laugh together briefly.

After the laughter dies down, Two-Tone says, "I belief it's you, Eddy, my old confidant. Where you been? You went MIA like the CIA on your BOI!"

"I know, Two-Tone. I took some time off to improve my health and my lifestyle," says Eddy.

"Well, to what do I owe the pleasure of this call, my dawg? And if its ladies you're looking for, Two-Tone is knocked out on the ten count. I'm just stuck with my main bitch, and she's all cracked out. But she still puts food on the table to my broken down stable," says Two-Tone.

"Well, sounds like I'm calling you at the right time," says Eddy. "I have a way we can both make some good money. I just need your help."

"My man Eddy, money! Now you're talking," says Two-Tone. "What do you need from me?"

Eddy says, "I need someone to take bread and water to a hide-out place where I have stashed three women. I'm giving them just enough nutrition to keep them alive."

Two-Tone is shocked. He knows just the right person for the job, but he doesn't reveal it before he expresses his opinion. "Eddy, what are you doing, man? You holding women captive and starving them?"

Eddy replies, "Yeah. So what? Are you in or out?"

Two-Tone thinks only about the money and goes with it. He tells Eddy that his bitch's brother is perfect for the job. He is a grimy, careless human being who can carry out the task for him. But Two-Tone insists on a monetary advance. He tells

Eddy that he must toss him a bone first, for good faith. Eddy agrees to Two-Tone's terms, and they go forward together.

Days later, Eddy is to meet up at his warehouse with the runner provided by Two-Tone. Eddy arrives first and waits outside the gates. Shortly after he arrives, a beat up pick-up truck pulls up, and a big six-foot monster of a man emerges. He looks like a kindred spirit, and that pleases him. Eddy introduces himself and instructs the wicked man how to carry out his task. The man is to come once a week and deliver a gallon of water and a loaf of bread to the individuals who are locked up inside. He is to do whatever is necessary if one tries to escape in the process, without using deadly force. Eddy hands the man an envelope filled with money and tells him that he is expecting things to go according to his plan. Eddy explains that half the money is to go to Two-Tone, and the man agrees to the terms.

A week goes by, and Eddy calls the runner to ensure that he is around and to inform him that it's feeding time. As soon as he disengages the call, he makes himself a hefty meaty sandwich.

Week after week, the runner makes his runs delivering bread and water without any interruptions from Eddy. In the meantime Eddy contacts Two-Tone to check on his situation. "Two-Tone, this is Eddy. I just wanted to see how things are going."

"Things are okay, but this money is not the type of money I was expecting, Eddy."

"I understand," says Eddy. "That was just an incentive. The real money is coming. But I need you to do your part now to guarantee we both get paid. Okay?"

"And where's that money coming from, Eddy?"

"I need you to contact some of your old counterparts from the underworld and find out if we can move these women for cash."

"Okay," says Two-Tone. "But I'm not promising anything. I might take them off your hands myself. I need girls."

"Just do it, Two-Tone," says Eddy, ending the call.

Two-Tone comments to himself, *This motherfucker has gone crazy!* But he is involved already, and he sees a potential for being back on top. Two-Tone complies and hits the streets. He knows just how cruel the streets are, and he knows just where to look for a millionaire buddy of his who goes by the name of Peter. He is known for having the magic dust and controlling his women with it. *Yeah!*

Two-Tone thinks. *Peter should have no problem taking these ladies off us.*

Two-Tone meets with Peter in front of his place of operation and lays out the skinny. Peter is pleased to hear that Two-Tone is headed back in the direction of making money but tells him no on the women. He tells Two-Tone that he is doing it all the wrong way.

While the two men meet, they are being surveilled by the police. Their conversation is being documented. After Two-Tone makes his way out of the vicinity, two police officer approach Peter and asked him if that was Two-Bit Tony he was just talking too. Peter replies, "No, man! That was just some washed-up bum asking for money."

One of the officers responds, "I think your lying,

Peter. That looked like Two-Bit Tony to us. And we're going to find out why he came to you."

Peter replies, "Good luck with that, man."

The officers says, "You're going down, Peter."

Peter replies "I'm so high in the sky I'm never coming down like a clown with a frown. You can't bust me if you wanna. I got you in my pocket not the other way around, sucka. Now get out of my face. I got dough to make."

The officer says, "You're right! I have kids to put though collage."

After receiving a no-go from Peter, Two-Tone Tony relays the news to Eddy. Eddy is slightly disappointed in Two-Tone's efforts but continues on with the feeding and transformation of his victims.

Two months pass, and Two-Tone's runner keeps doing his job according to plan. He keeps Eddy informed on the process. Eddy is pleased with the outcome. Two-Tone connects back with Eddy to check on things. Two-Tone insists that Eddy give the women to him. He will provide compensation after not being able to deliver on the sale to Peter. Eddy agrees and sets up a time to meet at his warehouse to conduct the transfer of the imprisoned women successfully into Two-Tone's possession.

Eddy tells Two-Tone not to bring his runner with him; he must come alone. Two-Tone replies, "Come on, Eddy! I need him for this. He's going to help us like he has been doing this entire time."

Eddy agrees to Two-Tone's demands and tells Two-Tone to bring his runner along. He mentions that guy gives him the creeps.

Two-Tone says, "Gives *you* the creeps? We're

fixing to go pick up some women that you've locked up and starved for months!"

Eddy laughs and says, "You're right. He's cool. I'm cool. Just make sure you're both there to meet me on time, and make sure you're not being tailed."

"Understood."

The following morning at daybreak, Eddy pulls up to his warehouse, parks his car outside the entrance gate, cranks the air conditioner, and calls Two-Tone. Two-Tone answers immediately, almost as if he has been up all night waiting for Eddy's call. "Hello."

"You have thirty minutes to get here. That freak that you're bringing along knows how to get here. Let's go!" says Eddy.

"I'm on my way," says Two-Tone

Two-Tone and his associate arrive on time.

Two-Tone pulls his car up next to Eddy's vehicle and tries to get Eddy's attention by waving him down. But Eddy seems to be preoccupied with loud music and snorting something up his nose multiple times. Finally, Two-Tone gets out and knocks on Eddy's window. Eddy is startled and grabs a gun but notices it is Two-Tone. He opens the car door and gets out.

Two-Tone says, "You knew I was coming. What's with the gun?"

"The gun's not for you. It's just for intimidation inside," says Eddy. He then hops out his car and lands on both feet, shaking his head left to right and up and down. After settling himself, Eddy steps up to Two-Tone and stares directly into his face. In a monotone voice, he says, "Now let's go see what these pigs look like." He points at Two-Tone's van and says, "Tell him to get out and come with us."

All three of them then walk through the entrance gate, and into the building. As they are walking through the building, Two-Tone says, "This place is fucked up, Eddy."

"I know. And I love it," Eddy replies. They reach the heavily secured entrance door to the room where Eddy's victims are imprisoned. Eddy turns to Two-Tone's associate and says, "Freak, did you bring your keys?"

Two-Tone's runner replies in a wicked dark voice, "Nobody told me to bring my keys."

"Never mind," Eddy says, "I have mine." He unlocks the extremely large padlock that secures the door and opens the door slowly. Light slowly drifts into the room and shines brightly on two incredibly skinny but beautiful young women, and one somewhat chubbier but cute young woman.

Eddy turns to Two-Tone and points to the women as he speaks. "That one's Paula, and that one's Michelle. Damn! They look different! But this one looks the same as the day I brought her here." Eddy turns to Two-Tone's associate and asks, "You never reported this back to me."

Two-tone's associate responds, "How was I supposed to know?'

Eddy replies, "Never mind. Tony, you and your freak take those two. I'll worry about this one myself." He indicates the still-overweight woman. "I have other plans for her."

Two-Tone and his associate successfully transport the two women to Tony's vehicle and exit the property, leaving Eddy alone there with the untransformed and less-desirable woman. Eddy walks further into the room and gets closer to his victim. He tries to sweet talk her by saying, "Do you remember me? I am the one who was going to take you out that one night, but we ended up here instead." Then he changes up his tone. "I think you starved those other women by not sharing the food provided to you all. You could have killed them!"

At this point, the words that are coming out of Eddy's mouth certify him as deranged. He is trying to blame an innocent person for what he has done. Eddy says, "I never got your name. Do you mind sharing it with me?"

"Fuck you! That's my name."

"I think *I* will fuck *you*. Now get up, take your clothes off, and bend over and grab your fucking cankles so that I can fuck your fat round butt just like I know you wanted me to the night I brought you here."

Out of fear, she complies with Eddy's wishes. Even in these devastating circumstances, she is still sexually attracted to Eddy, and she enjoys every minute of her punishment. When he is finished, she walks over to the corner of the room, lies down in a fetal position, and falls asleep. Eddy then makes a clean break for the exit, leaving her there to rot.

With the front money from Eddy, Two-Tone has been able to have his new women looking the part. He is now making thousands of dollars hand over fist. And lucky for Two-Tone, the two new women he has are actually enjoying their new lifestyle. With their new beauty treatments, makeup, and clothes, they are surprisingly loving the sex that they are having with all the men Two-Tone fixes them up with. Two-Tone is now back on top with a new wardrobe, jewels, a fancy car, and a fist full of money. He starts making appearances at his old hangouts and mingling with old counterparts. He also cuts Eddy in on the profits.

Months go by, and Two-Tone is gaining more success as time progresses, leaving him open for law enforcement to recognize his quick rise. He already has a history with the law, and he had been in the can a couple times in the past. But he is blind to their current attention on him until one night when he is out. He runs into Peter whom he had approached with the proposition of selling off Eddy's ladies. Peter tells Two-Tone that, after their meeting that day, the police approached him after Two-Tone had left. "They were asking questions about you, and they said that they were going to find out what was going on with you. Be careful,

Two-Tone. After that, Two-Tone immediately slows down his operation. Even though he is greedy, he plays it smart. He takes his girls and money and lies low for a while.

After so long trying to stay undetected, Two-Tone realizes the heat is on. He puts together the money he earned before he went into hiding and adds it to the money he was able to make while lying low. Then he sets the ladies free and goes on the lamb. But not before calling Eddy first.

The phone rings, and Eddy picks up. "Hello?"

"Eddy this is Two-Tone Tony. I'm just calling you to warn you the heat is on. They are coming for us Eddy."

"What are you worried about, Two-Tone ?"

"I know more than you know, Eddy. Get out now, man! I already let the ladies go."

"You did what!"

"I had to. I'm not a killer, Eddy."

"You fucked up, Two-Tone! I'm going to take care of the last one. Then I'm coming for you."

"Man, Eddy, you can't be talking to me like that. I was trying to be your friend, Eddy, but you know what? You are just some fat fucking punk that went crazy after your wife left you!" Two-Tone realizes his call is no longer connected. "Eddy! Eddy! Are you there?" There's no response from the other end.

Eddy has ended the call and dropped the phone on the floor. He thinks sadly to himself about what he has become. But he is still determined to take care of what he started. He pulls open a drawer and reaches inside for his gun. He tucks it into his waistband and leaves his house in haste, headed for his warehouse.

Eddy pulls up to the entry gate. Instead of getting out to unlock it, he rams right through it and drives his car across the parking lot all the way up to the door. Eddy gets out the car discombobulated. He leaves his car door open and the vehicle running. He quickly opens the door and goes inside, pulling out his gun and pointing it at the prison door as he runs toward it and his last remaining hostage. Eddy fumbles with the keys and drops them in the dirt as he tries to unlock the door. Out of frustration, he kicks them away. He cannot see where they went. In a rage, Eddy shoots the lock off the door. The sound wakes up the poor unnamed, diminished young lady inside. Eddy kicks the door wide open, causing a beam of light to shine on the slumped-down, malnourished young lady.

She looks up to the shadowy figure standing in

the doorway holding a gun. Eddy walks in slowly. All his adrenaline fades as he comes to the hard realization of what he has become. Eddy tells the girl, "You get up and get out of here." The girl is distraught and apprehensive. She takes her chances. She gets up slowly and walks toward the door. She passes by Eddy and makes her way out of the room.

Eddy drops to his knees and points the gun to his head. He thinks about Paula and wonders if there still might be hope. So he slowly lowers the gun from his temple and tosses it onto the floor behind him. He gradually stands up. A smile breaks out on his face. He turns around to leave but discovers that his prisoner is still there. Now she is standing in the doorway pointing his own gun at him. His smile turns to tears as he realizes his fate. He screams out for Paula one last time. But the word is cut off by ever last bullet in his gun. The unnamed survivor drops the weapon on the ground, after brutally killing Eddy. She stands over him and said, The entire world will know who I am after this."

THE END

Milton Keynes UK
Ingram Content Group UK Ltd.
UKHW041007111124
451035UK00002B/387